TWO BAD BOYS

A VERY OLD CHEROKEE TALE

RETOLD AND ILLUSTRATED BY

Gail E. Haley

DUTTON CHILDREN'S BOOKS • NEW YORK

To Tom Gomez, who climbed trees, posed, and taught me to laugh in Cherokee.

With special thanks to:
Annabelle Cucumber, Tom's grandmother; Jean Jones, who teaches children to dance;
Walker Calhoun, whose voice, music, and message have inspired me;
and for all the people of Cherokee who have shared their world with me most generously.

David Moore, of the North Carolina State Historical Preservation Office, supplied information
to help render the Stone Age lodge and corn storehouse. Cherokee translation and script were
contributed by Myrtle D. Johnson. Art, artifacts, and customs of the Cherokee people
were studied at the Quallah Museum and Cultural Center, and
Oconaluftee Village in Cherokee, North Carolina.

✦ ✦ ✦

ABOUT THE STORY

This is a traditional Cherokee legend as recorded by Swimmer, a famous Cherokee shaman and
storyteller. Born in 1835, he learned to read and write using the Cherokee alphabet, or syllabary,
developed by the tribe's leader, Sequoyah.

The powerful figure of the Father, or First Hunter—called Kanati in this story—appears in
many other myths. Kanati, with the wolf at his side as his hunting dog, has dominion over all the
animals, and sometimes he can control even the thunder.

His wife, Selu, is called Corn Mother, Old Mother, and even Great Mother. She is responsible
for the proper progression of the seasons and for the fertility of all crops. She protects and cares
for her children, even the ones as naughty as the two bad boys in this story.

Wild Boy features in the myths of many countries. Because this figure appears magically as a
half-grown child, he never seems to know right from wrong like children who are taught the rules
of their tribe or clan from their infancy. And probably Wild Boy wouldn't even care! We are told
that Wild Boy can never be tamed, so we expect mischief from him whenever he shows up.

This ancient story speaks to the naughty child in each of us, the one who urges us to do the
things we normally would not dare. It has survived among the Cherokee people since the time
long before the coming of the white man, when the great woods bison and the elk still roamed
the forests of North Carolina.

✦ ✦ ✦

Copyright © 1996 by Gail E. Haley   All rights reserved.
Library of Congress Cataloging-in-Publication Data
Haley, Gail E.
Two bad boys: a very old Cherokee tale/by Gail E. Haley.—1st ed.   p.   cm.
Summary: Boy finds his wild brother under the surface of the river and pulls him out onto land,
where Wild Boy begins to lead him astray into trouble.   ISBN 0-525-45311-3   1. Cherokee Indians—
Folklore.   2. Tales—Southern States.   [1. Cherokee Indians—Folklore.   2. Indians of North America—Folklore.
3. Folklore—United States.]   I. Title   E99.C5H2223   1996   398.2'089'975—dc20   [E]   95-21415   CIP   AC

Published in the United States 1996 by Dutton Children's Books, a division of Penguin USA
375 Hudson Street, New York, New York 10014
Printed in Hong Kong   First Edition
10 9 8 7 6 5 4 3 2 1

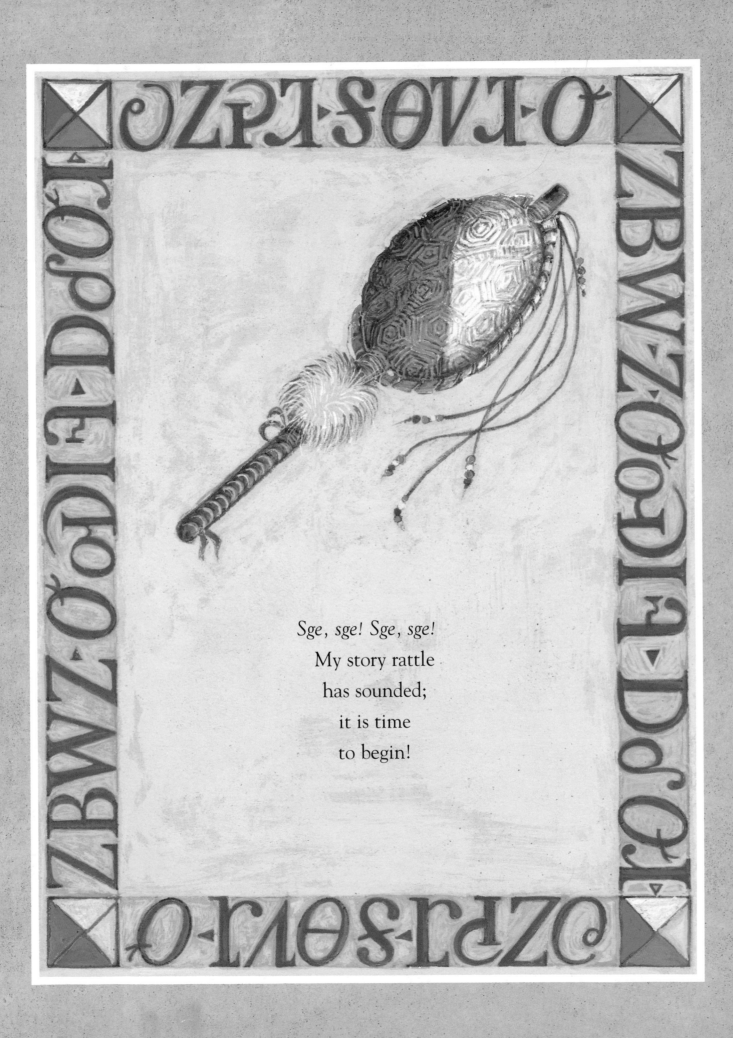

Sge, sge! Sge, sge!
My story rattle
has sounded;
it is time
to begin!

Listen! In the beginning, before there was a world of work, there was a family.

Kanati, First Hunter, returned every day from the hunt with Wolf at his heels. He always carried meat—sometimes a wild turkey, some rabbits, or a deer—over his shoulder.

Selu, Corn Mother, washed the meat and set it over the fire to cook. Then she would go to the storehouse to collect corn and beans in a beautiful basket she had woven.

Boy watched all that his parents did and listened carefully to the stories they told him.

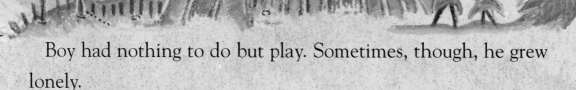

Boy had nothing to do but play. Sometimes, though, he grew lonely.

One day, as he built mud houses on the riverbank, he saw a boy beneath the surface of the water. He reached for the boy and touched his hand.

"Who are you?" he asked.

"I'm your wild brother," answered the other.

Boy was astonished. "If that is true, can you come and play with me?"

The strange boy came out of the water and played chunkie with Boy until dusk. Then the boy from the water went back into the river.

From that day on, the boy from the water came out of the river each morning to play with his brother. The boys thought up games of stickball, knucklebones, wrestling, and all the others that boys like to play. But at night the river boy always returned to the water.

Boy never said anything to his parents about his strange wild brother.

One day Mother Selu saw them playing together. That night over dinner she asked her son, "Who is that boy you were playing with today?"

"He says that he is my brother," Boy replied.

Kanati thought about this news. Then he said, "Tomorrow, ask this boy to wrestle with you. Then hold him tight and call us. We will come and catch him."

The next day, when the other boy came out of the river, Boy obeyed his father.

As soon as he had his brother pinned down, he called out to Selu and Kanati. They rushed from their hiding place and caught the other boy.

Ku! We all wish they had not; for although they had captured him, they could not tame him. And so they called him Wild Boy.

If there was mischief to be done, Wild Boy would think of it. And he always got his brother in trouble.

When he was hungry for sweets, he talked Boy into climbing the bee tree. Then he ate the honey while Boy nursed his stings.

He covered the smoke hole with tree limbs so that the lodge filled with smoke. Boy's eyes flowed with tears as he removed the branches.

Wild Boy got Boy to hold Wolf's pup so he could tie rattles to the animal's tail. When they released him, he overturned all of Selu's baskets and spilled the corn flour she was grinding.

"You bad boys!" she scolded them. "Go outside, and don't come back till dinnertime!"

One day Wild Boy said, "I wonder where Father goes to get the animals for our table. Let's follow him and see."

They followed their father to the river, and watched him cut reeds. He fitted a flint point to the end of each reed. On the other end he skillfully attached two feathers.

"What will he do with those?" asked Boy.

"I want to find out," said Wild Boy.

The brothers followed Kanati up a mountainside. At last he came to a giant stone in front of a cave. He pushed against it, and the stone rolled away.

Suddenly, out jumped a buck, and Kanati shot it with one of his arrows. Then he quickly rolled the stone back into place.

He gutted the deer, tied its legs together, and swung it across his shoulders.

"That is amazing!" exclaimed Wild Boy. Then they ran home ahead of their father, and pretended they had seen nothing.

After their evening meal of venison and corn cakes, Wild Boy patted his stomach and said, "That was a delicious meal. Where do you go, Father, to find such fine meat?"

"Ah, my son," said Kanati. "It is the way of the Hunter to know the secrets of the four-leggeds and the winged ones. It is the proper way of young boys to accept what they are given and not ask so many questions."

But Wild Boy could not stop asking questions. And he could not help planning and scheming. Now Wild Boy could not be happy with Boy's games. Finally, he took his brother aside.

"Let us go to the great stone as Father did and see what else is in the cave," he urged his brother.

"Father will be angry if we do that," said Boy.

But Wild Boy would not be silent until Boy finally agreed to his plan.

So the brothers went back to the mountainside to find the great stone.

The stone was heavier than they had imagined, and it took all their strength to roll it aside. No sooner had they moved it than out jumped a buck and a doe, a mountain sheep, and a buffalo, followed by all the other four-leggeds. The boys had to move out of the way to avoid being crushed by the stampede! Even turtle got away.

Birds escaped too. Turkeys, cranes, hawks, eagles, blue jays, crows, and all other winged creatures filled the sky, almost blocking out the light of the sun.

When Kanati saw them, he knew at once what had happened. He hurried to the cave and found his frightened sons.

"You two bad boys did not heed my words," he shouted. "Now I must go away. And you will have to track the animals and bring them down with bows and arrows. This you have brought on yourselves."

And he strode off to the Western Land of the Darkening Sun.

Now there was no time to play boys' games. The young brothers had to hunt every day to find enough meat just to stay alive.

They soon found out what it was like to feel hunger. The animals were too cunning for them, and most nights they went home empty-handed. As winter came on, they were cold as well as hungry.

Selu missed her husband, but she continued to look after the boys. She hung their frozen clothes by the fire, and gave them warm skins to wrap around themselves.

Each night, she would feed them corn and beans with a little jerky left over from Kanati's hunting. Boy spent many hours staring into the fire and regretting what they had done. The winter was long and hard.

One night in the spring, Wild Boy pulled his brother aside and whispered, "Where does Mother go to get the corn and beans? Let us follow her and see."

Boy did not want to listen to Wild Boy. He knew Selu would be angry if they followed her. But once again Wild Boy talked his brother into going along with his scheme.

They followed Selu to a small building of woven reeds and shingles that stood on stilts. They watched as she climbed a wooden ladder and disappeared inside.

"Come to the building with me, and let me stand on your shoulders so I can see what she does," Wild Boy pleaded.

Again, Boy did as Wild Boy asked. Standing on his brother's shoulders, Wild Boy was able to loosen a shingle and look inside.

Selu stood before a basket with her arms upraised and a golden light on her face. After a time she rubbed her stomach in the direction the sun goes round, and ears of corn came flying to shed their kernels into her basket. When it was half full, she rubbed her stomach in the opposite direction, and beans filled the basket to the top.

Oho, thought Wild Boy, I could easily do that.

When Selu bowed her head in gratitude, the boys ran home ahead of her. When she arrived, they acted as if they had seen nothing.

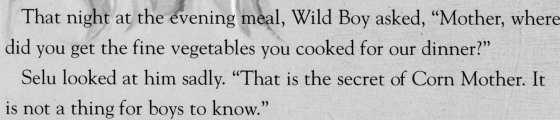

That night at the evening meal, Wild Boy asked, "Mother, where did you get the fine vegetables you cooked for our dinner?"

Selu looked at him sadly. "That is the secret of Corn Mother. It is not a thing for boys to know."

But next morning, as they left the lodge to hunt, Wild Boy said, "Let's go to the hut and gather food as we have seen Mother do."

"Oh, no, Brother, for I fear what will happen if we disobey again."

"But why should we always have to depend on Mother? This is not fair," Wild Boy argued. In the end, as always, he won. And Boy followed Wild Boy to the storehouse where Selu got the vegetables.

The boys had no difficulty in filling a basket as Mother had done. But when they came down the ladder, Selu was waiting for them.

"You two bad boys," she cried. "Because you have helped yourselves, our lives must change forever."

With a wave of her hand, the building pulled loose from the earth and flew away to the West.

"The corn and beans in your basket are all that you have left. From this time on, you must dig the earth, plant the seeds you hold, then tend and harvest the plants when they are ready," she told them.

Then Selu flew away to join her husband in the Western Land of the Darkening Sun.

Since that time, people have had to hunt for their meat, plant their vegetables, and *work* in this world. And all this was caused by those two bad boys.